For all of the mamas out there who have
buried in their confetti.

With love and thanks for my husband and
children, who made space for me to clear away mine.

ISBN 979-8-9858462-3-2 (Hardcover)
ISBN 979-8-9858462-4-9 (Paperback)
ASIN B0CNSKKSFW (Kindle eBook)

Published by Damselfly Reads Publishing
www.DamselflyReads.com

Mommy feels BIG THINGS

written by
Danielle L. Forbes

illustrations by
Anastasiia Bielik

Confetti! Confetti is for celebrating.
Confetti cannot be tamed.

And since our new baby came, Mommy's moods are often like confetti in the wind, spilling forth in disarray.

She tries to catch them all and hold them close, tries to keep her feelings tucked away. But like confetti, Mommy's feelings sometimes cannot be contained.

She can feel glad! She can feel angry! She can be worried or want to cry.
Mommy's moods sometimes seem to stomp and shout!
And all we can wonder is... **why?**

Before our new baby, Mommy's moods were gentle,
filled with smiles… Now we wonder, is it our fault that
they're rough, and, like done confetti… **scattered?**

Nope - no way! It is not our fault.
BIG THINGS happened, now Mommy just
has **BIG** feelings inside
she is working to sort out.

She has **BIG** feelings because everything within her cares, not because we did something bad.

Mommy will keep trying to express her feelings more calmly and clearly. Please be patient with her while she practices this.

We cannot change Mommy's **BIG** feelings, but there are **BIG THINGS** we can do to help while she practices feeling better through these uncomfortable, moody spells.

We can be gentle; we can be nice.
We can help give Mommy space
while she works to clear her mind.

When things are nice and tidy, it can feel just like a gift!

So we can pick up our **toys**...

and put away our **books**...

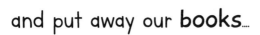

Or we can help Mommy while she prepares our food.

No, it is not our job to mend her, make
things perfect or repaired.

However, we can give her **lots of hugs** to
show her that we care!

Mommy's feelings might be **BIG**, but her love for us is even **BIGGER**. So let's take some deep breaths together, focus on that....**and remember:**

Being part of a family is **wonderful**.
It means having love, patience and grace.
Everyone is **important** and **special**.
That will never, ever change.

So while Mommy's moods might seem to travel everywhere right now, like **confetti** in the wind, please know, there is a truth that will always stay still:

We are forever inside Mommy's heart
and she loves us more than
we could ever know.

Post-Reading
FAMILY DISCUSSION

1. Is it okay to feel BIG THINGS?

2. In the story, is it the kid's fault that mommy feels BIG THINGS?

3. It's not a child's job to "fix" an adult. But there are BIG things we can do to help out. How did the kids in the story help their mommies so they could focus on feeling better?

4. What does self-care and good mental health look like for everyone in our family?

5. If someone in our family needs space for self-care, what is a good way they can signal that? (Tip: Determine the signal and follow-up actions together. Then practice it!)

For additional resources to encourage and facilitate self-care and mental health, please go to:

www.DamselflyReads.com

HELP OTHER FAMILIES LEARN ABOUT THIS BOOK WITH JUST A FEW CLICKS!

THE BIG THINGS SERIES

Danielle L. Forbes is an award-winning, Amazon best-selling children's book author and an award-winning educator with over 10 years of international teaching experience. Designing equitable learning experiences in literacy is her passion.

Anastasiia Bielik is an award-winning, Amazon best-selling children's book illustrator and 2D artist. A mom from Ukraine, she is inspired by nature and the wonders of childhood. She has been bringing author's ideas to life for nearly 10 years.

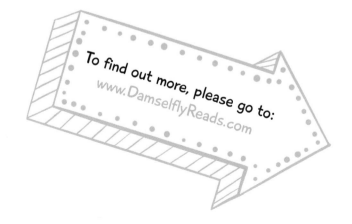

To find out more, please go to:
www.DamselflyReads.com

Printed in Great Britain
by Amazon